GEO

P9-DGY-484

Snap *books* ™

Fun Food for Cool Cooks

Wormy Apple Croissants

AND OTHER HALLOWEEN RECIPES

by Brekka Hervey Larrew

Capstone

Mankato, Minnesota

Snap Books are published by Capstone Press,
151 Good Counsel Drive, P.O. Box 669, Mankato, Minnesota 56002.
www.capstonepress.com

Library of Congress Cataloging-in-Publication Data
Larrew, Brekka Hervey.
　　Wormy apple croissants and other Halloween recipes / by Brekka Hervey Larrew.
　　p. cm. — (Fun food for cool cooks)
　　Summary: "Provides fun and unique recipes for a Halloween party, including nachos, cakes, and
cookies. Includes easy instructions and a helpful tools glossary with photos" — Provided by publisher.
　　Includes bibliographical references and index.
　　ISBN-13: 978-1-4296-1338-5 (hardcover)
　　ISBN-10: 1-4296-1338-6 (hardcover)
　　1. Halloween cookery. I. Title. II. Series.

TX739.2.H34L37 2008
641.5'68 — dc22   2007032854

Editor: Kathryn Clay
Designer: Juliette Peters
Photo Stylists: Kelly Garvin and Sarah Schuette

Photo Credits:
All principle photography in this book by Capstone Press/Karon Dubke
Capstone Press/TJ Thoraldson Digital Photography, cooking utensils (all)
David Larrew, 32

1 2 3 4 5 6 13 12 11 10 09 08

TABLE OF CONTENTS

PAGE 8

PAGE 12

PAGE 14

PAGE 16

PAGE 22

PAGE 24

INTRODUCTION

SEEING STARS

When choosing a recipe, let the stars be your guide! Just follow this chart to find recipes that fit your cooking comfort level.

EASY: ★ ☆ ☆
MEDIUM: ★ ★ ☆
ADVANCED: ★ ★ ★

Witches, goblins, and ghosts! Halloween is full of frightening sights. Thankfully, cooking yummy Halloween food shouldn't scare you. From witchy wands to edible eyeballs, this book has plenty of terrifying and tasty treats.

Are you planning a party with all your friends? Or do you just want a quick holiday snack? This book will help you prepare the ultimate frightening feast. So grab your cauldron and get cooking!

METRIC CONVERSION GUIDE

United States	Metric
¼ teaspoon	1.2 mL
½ teaspoon	2.5 mL
1 teaspoon	5 mL
1 tablespoon	15 mL
¼ cup	60 mL
⅓ cup	80 mL
½ cup	120 mL
⅔ cup	160 mL
¾ cup	175 mL
1 cup	240 mL
1 quart	1 liter
1 ounce	30 grams
2 ounces	55 grams
4 ounces	110 grams
½ pound	225 grams
1 pound	455 grams

Fahrenheit	Celsius
325°	160°
350°	180°
375°	190°
400°	200°
425°	220°
450°	230°

All good cooks know that a successful recipe takes a little preparation. Use this handy checklist to save time when working in the kitchen.

BEFORE YOU BEGIN

READ YOUR RECIPE

Once you've chosen a recipe, carefully read over it. The recipe will go smoothly if you understand the steps and techniques.

CHECK THE PANTRY

Make sure you have all the ingredients on hand. After all, it's hard to bake cookies without sugar!

DRESS FOR SUCCESS

Wear an apron to keep your clothes clean. Roll up long sleeves. Tie long hair back so it doesn't get in your way — or in the food.

GET OUT YOUR TOOLS

Sort through the cupboards and gather all the tools you'll need to prepare the recipe. Can't tell a spatula from a mixing spoon? No problem. Refer to the handy tools glossary in this book.

PREPARE YOUR INGREDIENTS

A little prep time at the start will pay off in the end.

- Rinse any fresh ingredients such as fruit and vegetables.
- Use a peeler to remove the peel from foods like apples and carrots.
- Cut up fresh ingredients as called for in the recipe. Keep an adult nearby when using a knife to cut or chop food.
- Measure all the ingredients and place them in separate bowls or containers so they're ready to use. Remember to use the correct measuring cups for dry and wet ingredients.

PREHEAT THE OVEN

If you're baking treats, it's important to preheat the oven. Cakes, cookies, and breads bake better in an oven that's heated to the correct temperature.

The kitchen may be unfamiliar turf for many young chefs. Here's a list of trusty tips to help keep you safe in the kitchen.

KITCHEN SAFETY

ADULT HELPERS

Ask an adult to help. Whether you're chopping, mixing, or baking, you'll want an adult nearby to lend a hand or answer questions.

FIRST AID

Keep a first aid kit handy in the kitchen, just in case you have an accident. A basic first aid kit contains bandages, a cream or spray to treat burns, alcohol wipes, gauze, and a small scissors.

WASH UP

Before starting any recipe, be sure to wash your hands. Wash your hands again after working with messy ingredients like jelly or syrup.

HANDLE HABITS

Turn handles of cooking pots toward the center of the stove. You don't want anyone to bump into a handle that's sticking off the stove.

USING KNIVES

It's always best to get an adult's help when using knives. Choose a knife that's the right size for both your hands and the food. It may be tough to cut carrots with a paring knife that's too small. Hold the handle firmly when cutting, and keep your fingers away from the blade.

COVER UP

Always wear oven mitts or use pot holders to take hot trays and pans out of the oven.

KEEP IT CLEAN

Spills and drips are bound to happen. Wipe up messes with a paper towel or clean kitchen towel to keep your workspace tidy.

Caramel apples are messy to make but fun to eat. This recipe lets you enjoy the great taste without the mess. Just roll your caramel apple up in a flaky crust and add some ooey, gooey worms.

DIFFICULTY LEVEL: ★ ★ ★
SERVING SIZE: 8
PREHEAT OVEN: ACCORDING TO PACKAGE

WORMY APPLE CROISSANTS

WHAT YOU NEED

● ● *Ingredients*

1 Granny Smith apple, peeled
1 (8-ounce) package crescent rolls
¼ cup caramel topping
8 gummy worms

● ● *Tools*

vegetable peeler   cutting board   paring knife

saucepan   colander   baking sheet

small bowl   mixing spoon   tablespoon

oven mitt   pot holder

drinking straw

1 Use a vegetable peeler to peel an apple. On a cutting board, slice apple into fourths with a paring knife. Cut out the core and dice the apple into small chunks.

2 Place the apple chunks in a small saucepan and cover with water. Cook over medium heat for 5 minutes or until the apples are soft. Use a colander to drain apples.

3 On an ungreased baking sheet, spread out triangles of crescent roll dough.

4 In a small bowl, use a mixing spoon to mix apples with the caramel topping. Drop 1 tablespoon apple mixture into the middle of each triangle.

5 Fold dough over the filling and continue to roll into a crescent shape. Firmly press the edges together.

6 Bake according to the package directions. Use an oven mitt or pot holder to remove the baking sheet.

7 When croissants have cooled, push a drinking straw through each croissant. Put gummy worms in the holes. Drizzle caramel sauce over each croissant.

8

Tasty Tip

These treats can be made a day ahead of time. Prepare the apple mixture the night before and refrigerate it in an airtight container. When you wake up, you'll be able to bake the croissants in no time.

9

How do witches cast spells? With their witchy wands, of course. These wands taste so good, you won't need a magic spell to make them disappear.

WITCHY WANDS

WHAT YOU NEED

●● *Ingredients*

30 caramels
1 tablespoon butter
2 teaspoons milk
1 (10-ounce) bag pretzel rods
¾ cup semi-sweet chocolate chips
sprinkles

●● *Tools*

baking sheet

microwave-safe bowl

mixing spoon

nonstick cooking spray

coffee mug

1 Coat a baking sheet with nonstick cooking spray.

2 Microwave the caramels, butter, and milk in a microwave-safe bowl for 30 seconds. Stir and microwave an additional 30 seconds.

3 Use a mixing spoon to cover the lower half of the pretzels with caramel. Place pretzels on the baking sheet and allow caramel to cool.

4 Put chocolate chips in a coffee mug and microwave for 30 seconds. Stir and microwave an additional 30 seconds or until chocolate has melted.

5 Dip pretzel into melted chocolate so that the bottom third is covered.

6 Cover the chocolate part of pretzels with colored sprinkles.

7 Place pretzels on the baking sheet and allow chocolate to cool at room temperature for 2 hours or in the refrigerator for 20 minutes.

Dip Tips

Chocolate dipping is fun, and it's not hard if you know what to do. Here are some quick tips:

1 Melted chocolate should be smooth and shiny, without lumps.

2 Dipping can be messy. You can also use a spoon to spread melted chocolate onto the pretzel.

3 If the chocolate starts to harden, just heat it in the microwave for a few seconds.

Who knew that eyeballs could be so tasty? Use green olives to give these deviled eggs a spooky Halloween makeover. Paint on red veins, and your eyeballs will be ready to serve.

DIFFICULTY LEVEL: ★ ★ ☆

SERVING SIZE: 24

EDIBLE EYEBALLS

WHAT YOU NEED

●● Ingredients

12 hard-boiled eggs
2 tablespoons mustard
¾ teaspoon seasoned salt
¼ teaspoon onion powder
½ tablespoon vinegar
⅓ cup sour cream
24 green olives, sliced
red food coloring

●● Tools

cutting board   paring knife   small bowl

fork   tablespoon

toothpick

1 Prepare and peel hard-boiled eggs (see Hard-boiled Egg Tips). On a cutting board, slice the eggs in half lengthwise using a paring knife.

2 Remove the yolks from the egg whites. Place just the yolks into a small bowl. Mash yolks with a fork.

3 Add mustard, seasoned salt, onion powder, vinegar, and sour cream to the small bowl. Mix well with the fork.

4 Spoon yolk filling back into each egg white.

5 To form the irises and pupils of the eyeballs, place a green olive slice in the center of each deviled egg.

6 Dip a toothpick into red food coloring. Use the toothpick to paint red lines that look like veins.

Hard-boiled Egg Tips

1 Place eggs in a saucepan. Add enough water to cover the eggs. Cook on high until water starts boiling (about 10 minutes).

2 Reduce to medium heat and cook an additional 5 minutes.

3 Use a slotted spoon to scoop out each egg. Place eggs in a bowl of ice water for 10-15 minutes.

4 After the eggs have cooled, tap them on a counter or table until the shells crack. Then peel off the shells.

13

Rather than carving pumpkins, you'll be gobbling them up.
Use orange and black frosting to make these pumpkin pie cupcakes
look like spooky jack-o'-lanterns.

DIFFICULTY LEVEL: ★ ★ ☆
SERVING SIZE: 24
PREHEAT OVEN: 350° FAHRENHEIT

PUMPKIN PIE CUPCAKES

WHAT YOU NEED

●● *Ingredients*

1 package yellow cake mix
1 teaspoon cinnamon
½ teaspoon nutmeg
1 (12-ounce) can evaporated milk
1 (15-ounce) can pumpkin
3 large eggs
2 tablespoons vegetable oil
1 (16-ounce) can cream cheese frosting
2 drops orange food coloring
1 tube of black decorating icing

●● *Tools*

cupcake liners

muffin pan

large mixing bowl

rubber scraper

electric mixer

mixing spoon

oven mitt

pot holder

small bowl

toothpick

1 Put cupcake liners into a muffin pan.

2 In a large mixing bowl, combine cake mix, cinnamon, and nutmeg. Stir together with a rubber scraper.

3 Add evaporated milk and canned pumpkin to bowl.

4 Add eggs and vegetable oil to bowl. Combine ingredients together with an electric mixer on medium speed for 2 minutes.

5 Spoon the batter into baking cups, filling each $^2/_3$ full. Bake for 25-30 minutes.

6 Use an oven mitt or pot holder to remove the cupcakes from the oven and cool for 20 minutes.

7 In a small bowl, mix frosting and food coloring with the rubber scraper.

8 Use the same scraper to frost each cupcake. Decorate with black icing to form eyes, a nose, and a mouth on each jack-o'-lantern.

Trusty Tip

To make sure your cupcakes are done, insert a toothpick into the center of one. If the toothpick comes out clean, the cupcakes are done. If the toothpick comes out with batter on it, let the cupcakes bake a few more minutes.

Soul Cake

Hundreds of years ago in England, people celebrated All Souls' Day two days after Halloween. Children went from house to house singing for treats. In return, they were given soul cakes. But these "cakes" tasted more like sweet breads.

These crunchy witch hats are fun to eat alone or with a big scoop of ice cream. Add a few candy touches, and your ice cream will look like a witch's face.

WICKED WITCH HATS

WHAT YOU NEED

●● Ingredients

⅓ cup flour
1 (18-ounce) package refrigerated
    gingerbread cookie dough
24 sugar cones
decorating icing in a variety of colors
sprinkles

●● Tools

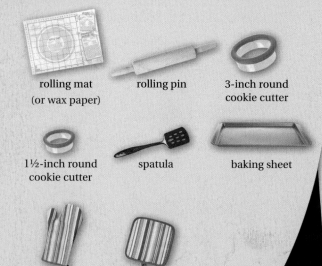

rolling mat   rolling pin   3-inch round
(or wax paper)   cookie cutter

1½-inch round   spatula   baking sheet
cookie cutter

oven mitt   pot holder

1 Dust a rolling mat and rolling pin with flour. Use rolling pin to flatten dough to about ¼ inch thick.

2 Use a 3-inch cookie cutter to cut out cookies. With a 1½-inch cookie cutter, cut a hole in the center of each cookie.

3 Use a spatula to move the cookie cutouts to an ungreased baking sheet. Place one sugar cone on top of each cookie so that it covers the hole. Press gently so the cone will stay in place. Bake according to the package directions.

4 Use an oven mitt or pot holder to remove the baking sheet from the oven. Allow cookies to cool for 10 minutes.

5 Squeeze decorating icing around the brims (where the cookie meets the cone) to form hatbands. Use additional icing and sprinkles to decorate cones.

Trusty Tip

If your cookie cutters are not the correct size for this recipe, find other kitchen items to use. Drinking glasses, tin cans, or empty spice jars all work well. When you find the items that will work best, make sure they're empty and clean.

Top it with Chocolate

For a sweeter taste, spread chocolate frosting over the cones and cookies. Then use chocolate sprinkles to decorate.

Your guests will get chills when you bring out these frozen treats. Instead of boos, you'll be hearing cheers when they taste these ghost pops.

DIFFICULTY LEVEL: ★ ★ ★
SERVING SIZE: 8

Spooky Ghost pops

WHAT YOU NEED

● ● *Ingredients*

4 bananas
2 cups white chocolate chips
black icing or chocolate sprinkles

● ● *Tools*

cutting board

paring knife

10 wooden
craft sticks

microwave-safe
bowl

plastic wrap

1 Peel bananas and place them on a cutting board. Cut bananas in half with a paring knife. Remove any stringy pieces.

2 Push a wooden craft stick through the end of each banana. Cover bananas in plastic wrap and freeze until firm (about 3 hours).

3 Melt white chocolate chips in microwave-safe bowl for 30 seconds. Stir and microwave again until chips are completely melted.

4 Dip bananas in melted white chocolate. Use black icing or chocolate sprinkles to add eyes and a mouth.

5 Cover bananas in plastic wrap and freeze until chocolate has set (about 20 minutes). Keep bananas in freezer until ready to serve.

19

Tasty Tip

Not a fan of white chocolate? No problem. Use semi-sweet chocolate chips instead. Dip the bananas in the melted chocolate and freeze until the chocolate hardens. Spread marshmallow creme on top of the chocolate. Add eyes and a mouth. Cover bananas in plastic wrap and freeze until marshmallow creme has set (about 20 minutes). Keep bananas in freezer until ready to serve.

Turn plain nachos into mini monsters with olive eyes, cheese noses, and tomato mouths. Dip your monsters into blood and guts (salsa). These nachos might sound scary, but they're delicious!

DIFFICULTY LEVEL: ★ ★ ★
SERVING SIZE: 4-5
PREHEAT OVEN: 350° FAHRENHEIT

BLOOD AND GUTS NACHOS

WHAT YOU NEED

●● *Ingredients*

1 cup cherry tomatoes
1 bag round tortilla chips
½ cup guacamole dip
¾ cup sliced black olives
1 cup cheddar cheese crumbles
½ cup red salsa
½ cup green salsa (optional)

●● *Tools*

cutting board   paring knife   baking sheet

tablespoon   oven mitt   pot holder

spatula

serving platter

1 On a cutting board, slice each tomato into 4 wedges with a paring knife.

2 Arrange chips on an ungreased baking sheet. Spread 1 tablespoon guacamole on each chip.

3 Add black olives, cheese crumbles, and tomatoes to each chip. Arrange so that each chip looks like a mini face.

4 Bake for 3-5 minutes. Use an oven mitt or pot holder to take the baking sheet out of the oven.

5 Using a spatula, immediately move chips to a serving platter. Serve with salsa.

Tasty Tip

If you're not a fan of guacamole, make brown monsters instead. Replace the guacamole with refried beans. You can also add onions, jalapeños, shredded chicken, or cooked hamburger to jazz up your nachos.

When you carve your jack-o'-lantern, don't forget to save the seeds. Toasted pumpkin seeds make a tasty travel snack. "Bone" appetite!

DIFFICULTY LEVEL: ★ ★ ☆
SERVING SIZE: 6
PREHEAT OVEN: 275° FAHRENHEIT

BONE-CRUNCHING PUMPKIN SEEDS

WHAT YOU NEED

● ● *Ingredients*

1 pumpkin
½ teaspoon salt
½ teaspoon garlic powder
1 tablespoon olive oil or butter

● ● *Tools*

mixing spoon

colander

small bowl

baking sheet

oven mitt

pot holder

paper towels

1 Use a large mixing spoon to dig out the pumpkin's pulp and seeds. Throw away as much pulp as you can without throwing away the seeds.

2 Place the seeds in a colander. Rinse with water to remove the remaining strings and pulp. Place clean seeds on a paper towel to dry.

3 In a small bowl, combine salt, garlic powder, and olive oil or butter with the mixing spoon.

4 Arrange 1 cup pumpkin seeds on a baking sheet and drizzle them with the salt mixture. Bake for 20-25 minutes or until the seeds are crunchy.

5 Use an oven mitt or pot holder to remove baking sheet from oven. Serve seeds while still warm or save for a snack later.

Tasty Tip

To make sweeter pumpkin pie seeds, replace the salt and garlic powder with ¼ teaspoon nutmeg, ¼ teaspoon cinnamon, and 1 teaspoon sugar.

Halloween History

People have been carving jack-o'-lanterns for more than 100 years! In Ireland, lanterns were first made by carving holes in turnips, not pumpkins. When this tradition was brought to America, people began to use pumpkins. Pumpkins were easier to find and easier to carve.

Do you need something to wash down all those Halloween sweets? Try Green Swamp Punch. It's fruity, fizzy, and tastes great served out of a cauldron!

DIFFICULTY LEVEL: ★ ☆ ☆
SERVING SIZE: 1 GALLON PUNCH

GREEN SWAMP PUNCH

WHAT YOU NEED

● ● *Ingredients*

1 (6-ounce) can frozen limeade concentrate
4 cups apple juice
1 (12-ounce) can mango, guava,
    or passion fruit nectar
3-5 drops green food coloring
4 cups ginger ale

● ● *Tools*

1 gallon pitcher

liquid measuring
cup

mixing spoon

1 Thaw and mix limeade as directed on package. Pour into a pitcher.

2 Measure apple juice and nectar with a liquid measuring cup. Add ingredients to the pitcher and mix well with a mixing spoon.

3 Add food coloring to the pitcher and stir.

4 Just before serving, add ginger ale to the pitcher.

24

25

This cool fruit salad uses Halloween's signature colors of orange and black. Even the yummy yogurt dip is orange!

DIFFICULTY LEVEL: ★ ☆ ☆
SERVING SIZE: 6

CHILLING FRUIT AND DIP

WHAT YOU NEED

●● *Ingredients*

1 cantaloupe, balled or sliced into bites
2 cups black seedless grapes
1 (6-ounce) carton blackberries
1 (8.5-11 ounce) can mandarin oranges
1 (8.5-11 ounce) can peaches
1 cup whipped topping
1 (6-ounce) carton orange or peach yogurt

●● *Tools*

cutting board   sharp knife   mixing spoon

mellon baller   large mixing bowl   colander

small bowl

1 On a cutting board, cut the cantaloupe in half with a sharp knife. Scoop out the seeds with a mixing spoon.

2 Use a melon baller to scoop out melon balls. Place melon in a large mixing bowl.

3 Add grapes and blackberries to the mixing bowl.

4 Drain oranges and peaches in a colander. Add these to the mixing bowl. Use a large mixing spoon to toss the fruits together.

5 In a small bowl, combine whipped topping and yogurt.

6 Serve fruit with dip on the side.

Cutting Edge

When cutting a cantaloupe, use a long, sharp knife to cut the fruit in half. Remove the seeds with a spoon and rinse the fruit. If you don't have a melon baller, slice the cantaloupe into wedges. Then switch to a paring knife. Remove the skin and cut the cantaloupe into bite-sized chunks.

TOOLS GLOSSARY

baking sheet — a large, flat, rectangular pan used for baking cookies and other items

colander — a bowl-shaped strainer used for washing or draining food

cookie cutters — hollow shapes made from metal or plastic that are used to cut cookie dough

cupcake liners — disposable paper or foil cups that are placed into a muffin pan to keep batter from sticking to the pan

cutting board — a wooden or plastic board used when slicing or chopping foods

electric mixer — a hand-held or stand-based mixer that uses rotating beaters to mix ingredients

fork — an eating utensil often used to stir or mash

liquid measuring cup — a measuring cup with a spout for pouring

melon baller — a kitchen tool with a rounded end used for scooping out balls of melon or other fruit

microwave-safe bowl — a non-metal bowl used in microwave ovens

mixing bowl — a sturdy bowl used for mixing ingredients

mixing spoon — a large spoon with a wide, circular end used to mix ingredients

muffin pan — a pan with individual cups for baking cupcakes or muffins

oven mitt — a large mitten made from heavy fabric used to protect hands when removing hot pans from the oven

paring knife — a small, sharp knife used for peeling or slicing

pitcher — a container with an open top and a handle that is used to hold liquids

pot holder — a thick, heavy fabric cut into a square or circle that is used to remove hot pans from an oven

rolling mat — a flat, plastic surface used when rolling out dough

rolling pin — a cylinder-shaped tool used to flatten dough

rubber scraper — a kitchen tool with a rubber paddle on the end

saucepan — a deep pot with a handle

sharp knife — a kitchen knife with long blade used to cut ingredients

small bowl — a bowl used for mixing a small amount of ingredients

spatula — a kitchen tool with a broad, flat metal or plastic blade at the end, used for removing food from a pan

tablespoon — an eating utensil often used to stir or scoop

vegetable peeler — a small tool with two blades used to remove peels from vegetables and fruits

wooden craft sticks — small flat sticks with rounded ends

GLOSSARY

cauldron (KOL-dren) — a large kettle, often associated with witches' brews

dice (DISSE) — to cut something into small cubes

drizzle (DRIZ-uhl) — to let a substance fall in small drops, like a light rain

dust (DUHST) — to lightly sprinkle

nectar (NEK-tur) — a sweet liquid found in many flowers

set (SET) — to harden

READ MORE

Blair, Beth L. and Jennifer A. Ericsson. *The Everything Kids' Halloween Puzzle & Activity Book: Hours of Spine-tingling Fun.* Avon, Mass.: Adams Media, 2003.

Court, Rob. *How to Draw Halloween Things.* Doodle Books. Chanhassen, Minn.: Child's World, 2007.

Mass, Wendy. *Celebrate Halloween.* Celebrate Holidays. Berkeley Heights, N.J.: Enslow, 2006.

INTERNET SITES

FactHound offers a safe, fun way to find Internet sites related to this book. All of the sites on FactHound have been researched by our staff.

Here's how:

1. Visit *www.facthound.com*
2. Choose your grade level.
3. Type in this book ID **1429613386** for age-appropriate sites. You may also browse subjects by clicking on letters, or by clicking on pictures and words.
4. Click on the **Fetch It** button.

FactHound will fetch the best sites for you!

ABOUT THE AUTHOR

Brekka Hervey Larrew began cooking with her mother when she was a little girl, mainly because she loved to eat (and still does). As a teenager, she held elaborate seven-course dinner parties for friends and relatives. Larrew baked as many varieties of cookies as she could find in recipe books. She has experimented with multicultural cooking and has spent a lot of time perfecting the art of baking pies.

Larrew taught elementary and middle school for 12 years. Currently, she stays home with her two children, both of whom help out in the kitchen. She lives in Nashville.

INDEX